Dear Parents:

Congratulations! Your child is taking
the first steps on an exciting journey.
The destination? Independent reading!

STEP INTO READING® will help your child get there. The program offers
five steps to reading success. Each step includes fun stories and colorful
art or photographs. In addition to original fiction and books with favorite
characters, there are Step into Reading Non-Fiction Readers, Phonics Readers
and Boxed Sets, Sticker Readers, and Comic Readers—a complete literacy
program with something to interest every child.

Learning to Read, Step by Step!

Ready to Read   Preschool–Kindergarten
• big type and easy words • rhyme and rhythm • picture clues
For children who know the alphabet and are eager to
begin reading.

Reading with Help   Preschool–Grade 1
• basic vocabulary • short sentences • simple stories
For children who recognize familiar words and sound out
new words with help.

Reading on Your Own   Grades 1–3
• engaging characters • easy-to-follow plots • popular topics
For children who are ready to read on their own.

Reading Paragraphs   Grades 2–3
• challenging vocabulary • short paragraphs • exciting stories
For newly independent readers who read simple sentences
with confidence.

Ready for Chapters   Grades 2–4
• chapters • longer paragraphs • full-color art
For children who want to take the plunge into chapter books
but still like colorful pictures.

STEP INTO READING® is designed to give every child a successful
reading experience. The grade levels are only guides; children will progress
through the steps at their own speed, developing confidence in their reading.
The F&P Text Level on the back cover serves as another tool to help you
choose the right book for your child.

Remember, a lifetime love of reading starts with a single step!

For Clark Henley

Copyright © 1988 by James Marshall

All rights reserved. Published in the United States by Random House Children's Books, a division of Penguin Random House LLC, New York. Originally published in hardcover in the United States by Dial Books for Young Readers, an imprint of Penguin Random House LLC, New York, in 1988.

Step into Reading, Random House, and the Random House colophon are registered trademarks of Penguin Random House LLC.

Visit us on the Web!
StepIntoReading.com
rhcbooks.com

Educators and librarians, for a variety of teaching tools, visit us at
RHTeachersLibrarians.com

Library of Congress Cataloging-in-Publication Data is available upon request.
ISBN 978-0-593-43268-6 (trade) — ISBN 978-0-593-43269-3 (lib. bdg.)

Printed in the United States of America
10 9 8 7 6 5 4 3

This book has been officially leveled by using the F&P Text Level Gradient™ Leveling System.

FOX ON THE JOB

by James Marshall

Random House 🏠 New York

Fox liked to show off
for the girls.
"Oh my!" said the girls.

One day Fox showed off just
a little too much.

"Look out!" cried the girls.

"Look out!"

Fox was saved,

but his bike

was a wreck.

"That's all right,"

he told the girls.

"I'll just ask my mother

for a new one."

"Now, see here, Fox," said Mom.

"I'm not made of money.

You will just have to get a job

if you want a new bike."

"A job!" said Fox.

"There must be some other way."

And he went to his little sister.

"Louise, dear," said Fox.

But Louise would not help.

"I'll scream!" she said.

"I won't forget this,"
said Fox.

"Who needs a bike, anyway?"
said Fox.

Just then Carmen rode by.

"Tra-la!" sang Carmen.

"That does it!" said Fox.

And he went to look for a job.

NEW
SHOES

Downtown, Fox saw a sign

in a window.

HELP WANTED! NOW!

"I'm in luck," said Fox.

He went inside.

"Help is here!" he said.

"Not so fast," said the owner.

"Can you sell shoes?"

"Of course I can," said Fox.

"Are you honest?" said the owner.

"Oh yes!" said Fox.

"Well," said the owner.

"Let's give it a try.

You can start right away."

And he went to eat his lunch.

Fox kept himself busy.

"What an easy job," he said.

"Excuse me," said a lady.

"Can you help me?"

"That's what I'm here for,"
said Fox.
"I need some shoes,"
said the lady.
"Some pretty, little, pink ones."
Fox looked at the lady's feet.

"You can't mean it," he said.

"We may not *have* shoes that big.

Those are the biggest feet!"

"Well, I *never*!" cried the lady.

"What seems to be the trouble?"

said the owner.

"He said I have big feet!"
cried the lady.
"There, there," said the owner.
"Your feet are tiny."
And he turned to Fox.
"This is not the job for you."
"Well, I *never*!" said Fox.

THE HAUNTED HOUSE

Fox walked by

the amusement park.

"Too bad I don't have money

for a few rides," he said.

"I heard that," said Mr. Jones,

who ran the park.

"Perhaps you would like a job?"

"You don't mean it!"

said Fox.

Mr. Jones put Fox to work
at the Haunted House.
"What's inside?" said Fox.
"Oh, it's very scary,"
said Mr. Jones.

Fox's first customers were Carmen
and her little brother Clark.

"A ticket for the kid," said Carmen.

"Aren't you going in?" asked Fox.

"It's not scary enough," said
Carmen.

Fox and Carmen waited and waited.

"What's taking that kid so long?"
said Fox.
"Maybe he got lost," said Carmen.
"Why don't you go inside
and look for him?"

"I beg your pardon?" said Fox.

"You aren't scared, are you?"

said Carmen.

"Me, scared?" said Fox.

And he went into the

Haunted House.

Inside it was really something.

"Welcome to the Haunted House!"
cried a skeleton.

"I'm coming to get you!"
cried a ghost.

"Boo!" cried a vampire.

Poor Fox was as white as a sheet.

"Hi, Fox!" said Clark.

"I'll show you how to get out."

"For shame!" said Fox to Mr. Jones.
"That's no place for little kids!
I quit!"

"Oh, pooh," said Mr. Jones.
"They love it!"

PIZZA
TIME

Fox saw his friend Dexter
coming out of the pizza parlor.
"You can't fire *me*," said Dexter.
"I quit!"
"Fine," said the boss.
"Maybe my next delivery boy
won't eat up all the pizza!"
Dexter left in a huff.
And Fox stepped inside
the pizza parlor.

"Do you have a job for me?"
asked Fox.

"Do you like pizza?" said the boss.

"I prefer hot dogs," said Fox.

"Excellent," said the boss.

"Are you fast on your feet?"

"Like the wind," said Fox.

"Excellent," said the boss.

"Take this pizza over to
Mrs. O'Hara.

She has been waiting a long time."

Fox was out the door in a flash.

On Homer's Hill

Fox picked up speed.

"I'm the fastest fox in town,"

he said.

At that moment Louise came

around the corner.

She was taking her pet mice

to the vet for their shots.

It was quite a crash!

Fox, Louise, and everything else
went flying.

They saw stars.

"Now you've done it!" said Fox.

"You've made me late.

I'll really have to step on it!"

And he hurried away.

Louise went to the vet's.

Doctor Jane opened the box.

"Where are your pet mice?"
she said.

"This looks like a pizza."

"Uh-oh," said Louise.

Fox knocked on Mrs. O'Hara's door.

"It's about time," said Mrs. O'Hara.

"I'm having a party.

And we're just dying for pizza."

"It will be worth the wait," said Fox.

"Pizza time!" said Mrs. O'Hara
to her friends.
She opened the box.

Back at the pizza parlor

the boss was hopping mad.

"Mrs. O'Hara just called," he said.

"And you are fired!"

"Didn't she like the pizza?" said Fox.

A
BRIGHT
IDEA

"This just isn't my day," said Fox.
"But I'm not giving up.
I'll think of something."

Just then he came to
a furniture store.
And suddenly he had a bright idea.

"Business is bad, Fox,"
said the owner of the store.
"I can't give you a job."

"Maybe you can," said Fox.
And he told the owner his
bright idea.

Later that day Carmen and Dexter
were out for a stroll.

"Look at that," said Dexter.

A large crowd was standing
in front of the furniture store.

"I can't see," said Carmen.

"Lift me up."

Dexter lifted Carmen above
the crowd.

"What is going on?" said Dexter.

"It's Fox!" shouted Carmen.

"What a great bed!" said someone.

"I want one!" said someone else.

"What a great idea!" said the boss.

But Fox was already sound asleep—

and dreaming of his new bike.